I0549560

# Duke's Heartbreak
# & other stories

## Beatrice Holloway

**TSL Publications**

First published in Great Britain in 2023
By TSL Publications, Rickmansworth

Copyright © 2023 Beatrice Holloway

ISBN: 978-1-915660-41-1

The right of Beatrice Holloway to be identified as the author of this work has
been asserted by the author in accordance with the UK Copyright, Designs and
Patents Act 1988.

All characters and events in this publication, other than those clearly in the
public domain, are fictitious and any resemblance to actual persons, living or
dead, is purely coincidental.

All rights reserved. No part of this publication may be reproduced, stored in a
retrieval system or transmitted, in any form or by any means without the prior
written permission of the publisher, nor be otherwise circulated in any form of
binding or cover other than that in which it is published and without a similar
condition being imposed on the subsequent buyer.

Cover courtesy of : https://unsplash.com/photos/HX_yGEB2evI
https://unsplash.com/photos/Iy9wIDKL4YU
https://unsplash.com/photos/TgQ9yKswXOQ

# Contents

# BOOKS BY BEATRICE

## Rhys series
1. Training a Greyhound and Other Troubles
2. Urgent! Pocket Money Required
3. Disasters and Delights of Family Celebrations
4. Enormous Responsibilities
5. The Sometimes Society
6. When Rhys Fell Out a Tree
7. A Question of Girls

## Towing Path Tales
1. Towing Path Tales
2. More Towing Path Tales
3. A Particular Year

## Adult
1. A Man from the North
2. Archie's Children
3. Elusive Destiny
4. Facts, Folklore and Feasts of Christmas (non-fiction)
5. Retired? You must be joking

## Plays
1. A Certain Monday
2. Connie's Lovely Boy
3. From Commoner to Coronet
4. Governed by Magpies
5. In Less than Ten Minutes
6. Plays for Young Actors

## Poetry
1. The Promise and other Poems

# Duke's Heartbreak

Tonight I resigned from my job. From now on I shall play dumb, refuse to obey and then they will have to retire me. I really loved my work until tonight. Never again do I want to be tested in such a cruel manner.

I don't remember my mother as we were parted when I was a six weeks old pup. What I do remember was being tucked inside Mike's zip-up jacket.

Mike would have been about fourteen years of age then, 'All arms and legs,' his mother often said. When I came to him, he was shy and lonely, no real friends to speak of and had braces on his teeth which didn't help his shyness. He was so quiet but I knew he loved me.

Best of all for me, was his smell, I'd know it anywhere. It was a scent I would go to the ends of the earth for. It was very special to me.

From his smell I could guess his moods. I knew his PE days and I knew when he played football. I used to snuffle around his school bag. I could tell by the boots or trainers what the day's sport would be.

I knew when he was happy. Mostly when we were in the woods playing hide and seek. Of course, I always found him quickly, it was that scent of his that gave him away. I knew when he was cross, when he came home from school, a door would slam, but he was never cross with me. Sometimes I knew he was upset by the drag of his feet on the floor. I used to prick my ears up and learned it was something to do with teachers and exams.

Mike would carry me about in his jacket when I was small, unzipping it so that my head would poke out. He told everyone my name was Duke. He told them about my family tree and about my special food and our games. My bed was a cardboard box in the kitchen, or so mother thought but it was at the bottom of Mike's bed I liked best. It was warmer and there was his lovely scent.

We went for long walks through fields and woods where I enjoyed a magic of smells. I chased everything and anything that moved. Mike would laugh and call me a 'silly lump' when I returned to him. My tongue would be hanging out and dripping, my tail wagging and my coat wet from the long grass. Sometimes I'd have a swim in the rushing river.

Our parting just a year later was a sad one for me. 'Mike,' said his mother tersely, 'has new friends.' He often came home too late to walk or feed me. Mother would slam my food bowl down on the floor in a temper. My water bowl wasn't filled very often. My coat became matted and I also had a nasty smell about me so Mike's mother said, and made a big fuss about it although I didn't notice it.

Quite often I was able to escape through an open door. Straight away I headed for the woods. The turning point came when I caught my nose on a barbed wire. This happened when I belly-crawled under it chasing a fox. It was only a small nick, but bled quite a lot. I made my way home and mother was upset at the sight of my bleeding so much. I was lovingly wrapped in a towel (Mike's scent was on it), and taken to the vet. He said it was only a little scratch and dabbed at it with a wet soft white ball. This had something on it which stung me. I growled and was hard put not to bite him. As it was I showed him my teeth and growled another warning. After a short while, the stinging faded. The vet quickly, but gently, ran his hands over my body and legs and then spoke quite sharply to Mike's mother. I growled another warning. He told her I was a lively and bright dog and that I needed exercise and work. He asked her how I had got to this poor state. After hearing the reasons, he nodded a bit and then said he thought I should go to a local Police Training School.

So began my new life. It meant leaving my beloved Mike. To be honest I loved every moment of being a police dog. To start with, I seemed never to make the right moves for the pointing fingers and stern, firm voices. Soon I learned through warm praise, a rub under the chin and the odd biscuit. I was shown off and showed off at all sorts of shows.

I liked my handler, Tom, but I still ached at times for Mike. Sometimes his scent was faintly in the wind, but of course, my training kept me at Tom's side. My work was catching criminals –

whatever that meant. I would have to follow a scent given me by Tom. The scent always had a smell of fear about it. It was quite simple work really.

This evening Tom and I were called out to follow a trail. It was Mike's, mixed with the usual smell of fear. I was so excited. I ran as fast as I could, I was to be with Mike. In no time at all I found him, crouched at the foot of a high wall. I cornered him as my training came to the fore and as Tom wanted. I could not bring myself to hold him in my jaws. Mike put his hand out. I sniffed at the lovely scent that had bonded me to him not so long ago. He put his arms around my neck and lowered his head onto mine and whispered, 'Oh, Duke.' I licked his face and tasted his salty tears.

As Tom led Mike away I knew I had done my job well, almost to the rule book, but in doing so my heart was broken.

THE END

# *Stowaways*

We are boat people and live on narrowboats. We deliver all sorts of cargo to different parts of the country, mostly between London and Manchester. Every time we are about to cast off after loading the latest goods, my Pa would yell out to me or my brother Ned, 'Go search the back for any stowaways and be quick about it.' He is always keen to be on the way smartly so that he could get a return cargo and then get paid and tout around for a new load. Always, as if he was having a rethink, Pa would then shout, 'Ned, you go and see to Nellie. Bert...' that's me, 'can go and look himself.' Pa would mutter something under his breath before adding, 'Any creature who thinks it can have a free ride with board and lodgings is going to be very unlucky.' Pa meant vermin, rats or mice that could spoil a cargo of sugar or flour or vegetables in next to no time. If we delivered damaged cargo the overseer would dock the cost out of Pa's money.

Nellie is our towing horse and Ned stuffs her nosebag with fresh hay and makes sure the tow rope and harness are secure and not chaffing her. We all knew if Nellie didn't get her feed she would be stubborn and not make any effort to pull the boat along. Pa didn't believe in beating dumb animals, 'A bit of bribery don't come amiss,' he always said as he gave her a slap on her rump. Bless her, Nellie knew the routine as well as ourselves once we were underway.

Besides Pa, Ned, and myself were Ma and four more children. Pa keeps threatening to farm them out, but hasn't the heart to do so. Also, he had upset Ma greatly when my sister, Lizzie was boarded out. Ma wasn't a one for crying but she was very down for weeks. Even so we are very crowded for space, but we manage fairly nicely.

The best way I found to seek out pests is to crawl among the sacks or wooden chests and beat each one soundly. I enjoy doing this pretending I am a soldier seeking out the enemy. Ma always laughs, 'You do get up to some funny larks,' she says. I keep beating until the creatures burst out of their hiding places and then anyone not working chases them and throws them overboard.

One day I found a mother hedgehog and her baby and I wondered how they had got onto the boat. We all jumped on or off the boat and the board was only used when Pa legged us through a tunnel. He always grumbles about doing this especially as some tunnels are over two miles long. As soon as Ned, my brother, was fourteen he had to help. He didn't mind, because he is always saying that one day he'd get his own boat so he must learn everything. Ned will soon be eighteen or thereabouts. Pa says he was born around 1895 or 1896 but he wasn't sure. I'm round about thirteen so I'm told. When I ask about my birthday the answer is always the same from Ma and Pa. 'Around the time apples ripen and night times is early.'

I wasn't sure what to do about the hedgehogs, but Ma got a shovel, scooped them up and threw them onto the bank. I was glad she didn't throw them in the water. 'If we was gypsies,' Ma told me, 'we'd eat them.' I didn't fancy that idea at all.

There was one stowaway we did keep – a kitten. She must have sneaked on when we were moored up at the loading dock. She was certainly curious enough to explore everything around her. She was so pretty, a tabby with green eyes and she seemed to dance on her dainty paws as she tried again and again to catch a butterfly. I loved her immediately and took her to ma. Ma put down a dish of water for her. The little uns pestered Ma, saying over and over again in turn, 'Can we keep her?' Ma shook her head.

'Please,' I begged.

I could see she was reluctant to say no. 'No, better not, your Pa won't have it,' she told us.

When Pa came aboard for his supper that evening, he picked the kitten up and spoke softly to her and she purred back as if answering him. Everyone was astounded. Very carefully, I had to be very careful as Pa had a fearsome temper, I asked, 'Can we keep her, Pa?' At first I thought he hadn't heard me as he went on stroking and talking to the kitten.

'Had a little kitten like you when I was a lad,' he told her. He looked around at the family and smiled. 'Of course we'll keep her.' He put her on the floor and she wound herself around his legs. 'She'll make a good mouser. Help Bert a bit, she will.' We called her Puss and she stayed with us for many years.

When she grew up a bit, and knew, 'What's what,' as Ma said, she produced a litter of kittens a number of times. Pa would sell them and buy Ma a gift and a few sweets for the rest of us. I think Ned would have liked a bit of baccy but Ma said he wasn't old enough. He winked at me as he'd been smoking since he was eight years old.

It was one of those really hot days when everything seemed to slow down or stop. The little uns were asleep in the shade of a shelter made from a tarpaulin Pa had put up. I was lying on my stomach on the cabin roof in the sun, drowsy and waiting to be called to help at the next lock. My eyelids were heavy and closed against the sun's glare. We'd left Stoke with a cargo of fine china about three hours ago and were bound for London. As everything was crated in wooden containers, I didn't bother too much searching for stowaways, Puss wandered about but she soon gave up.

I lifted my head, opened my eyes and saw a slight movement. A corner of the rainproof cover over the crates had moved. There was no breeze, no movement of air, but I couldn't be sure. I kept watch and after a few moments the corner was lifted again and was being lifted by a human hand! I couldn't believe it. Whatever I did now would cause ructions. If I called out to Pa, he would beat me for not looking properly and the stowaway would be thrown overboard.

I decided to investigate. I looked around, Pa was steering and looking straight ahead and Ned was walking beside Nellie. I could tell he was having a smoke as his cupped hand behind his back gave me a clue. Ma was sitting on the step her head resting on the hatch frame. She had fallen asleep and her knitting was in her lap. Silently, I lowered myself down onto the deck and crept to where I'd seen the movement. If it was a tramp, I would have to call for help and dad would sort things out. I didn't know whether to pull the cover back sharply or ease it up carefully. I lifted it gently.

I don't know who was more surprised, the girl crouched between two crates or myself. She whimpered, and I whispered, 'Be quiet or we'll both be in trouble.' I motioned to her to go further back and I crept in beside her. I had a thousand questions to ask her.

It was stifling and dark and I carefully raised the hem of the tarpaulin. This gave us a little air and some light. I looked at the girl and saw she was about fifteen or so. Her pretty face was wet with sweat or maybe tears, her black hair a tangle and her dress dusty and torn.

'What are you doing here?' I hissed at her. 'You shouldn't be here. How did you get aboard?' She covered her face with her hands and began to cry and as this turned into choking sobs, I found myself begging her to be quiet. I was so afraid that if she were discovered I'd get a lashing from the wide leather belt around pa's waist. I'd seen him use this on Ned once, I don't know what for, but Ned was black and blue for days. After a moment or two, she settled down.

'What's your name?' I whispered.

'Martha.'

'Well, Martha, you can't stay here. You'll have to get off at the next lock.'

Her big eyes looked into mine. 'I got to get to London.'

'London!' I almost exploded. 'That's days without food or water.'

'I got some food,' she answered. 'I got a loaf and some cheese.'

'That won't last a week.' I was stunned. 'What about water? You can't go that long without water.'

'I thought it might rain.'

'Well, it ain't going to rain today, that's for sure.'

I didn't know what to do. She had to go, but how? All very well saying get off at the next lock, but there might be folk about. If Pa saw her...

'What made you run away? You're running away from something I can tell.'

Martha gave a sniff. 'My uncle,' she murmured. 'He...' she stopped for a moment.

'Go on. Your uncle... what?'

'He intends to marry me off to a bargeman, said he promised the man.' That was bad news. Few boatmen get on with barge people. Some have a reputation of bullying and other unpleasant doings.

'But what about your Ma and pa? What do they say?'

'They died of a fever when I was little and my uncle – he became my family.' Again she hesitated. I heard her sigh. 'He was always telling me he didn't want me, I was a nuisance, eating the food meant for his own kids. I had the job of looking after them. They were alright, I think they liked me.' She was quiet for a moment. 'All the time as I was growing up he hated me.'

'What about your aunt? Didn't she do anything to help you?'

'She wasn't very strong and was mighty afraid of him.'

'So now he intends to get you married to get rid of you.'

'Yes.'

I began to feel sorry for her. Boat people might see someone they liked a couple of times, at a lock say, or inn and that was that. They got married and as far as I could tell, it seemed to work out pretty well.

'Do you know the bargeman? Do you like him?'

Martha pressed her lips together and her chin jutted out. 'I hate him. He's had two wives already and he's very old.' I could tell she had a bit of a temper on her.

'My uncle is sure to come looking for me,' she whispered.

Here was another problem. In my mind I thought I might have to choose between pa's hiding or the fists of an irate uncle – maybe even both. We sat in the semi darkness each with our own problems. There must be a way, I kept telling myself but how?

I nearly jumped out of my skin when I heard Pa shout, 'Bert, get yourself handy with the windlass, before I lose my temper.' We were at the lock and I struggled to get out. Thankfully Pa didn't see me and asked, 'Where the devil you been?' I told him I had fallen asleep and as cuffed me around the head, he yelled, 'Sleep at night, work in daylight. Understand?' He handed me the windlass and I leapt onto the towpath to escape then onto the lock to begin winding.

While I waited for the next chore, I looked around and realised that there were far too many people about. The lockkeeper's wife was leaning over the cottage gate, there were children in the garden and there were onlookers watching the boat descend. Ma had woken up and had jumped onto the towpath with the large kettle in her hand looking for water as Pa liked his mug of tea every hour. Ned was deep in conversation with a very well dressed young lady, spinning her some yarn I fancy. It would be the same at every lock. I just hadn't noticed people at locks before. I knew it would be impossible for Martha to leave without being seen at any lock. I must think of another plan, a secret plan so that Martha's uncle would never find her and a plan that meant that I, too, wouldn't get caught.

It was after supper before I was able to get back to Martha. We had moored up and eaten and I decided to sleep outside the cabin. Ma had to cook of course, but coupled with the day's sun and the heat from the stove, being inside was unbearable. As soon as I thought everyone was asleep, Pa snoring and Ma muttering in her sleep. I crept under the tarpaulin and whispered Martha's name. I sensed her stirring. 'Were you asleep?' I whispered.

'Sort of, but I am so hot.'

'Everyone's sleeping. You could come out for a little while. Get some air.' As soon as I said the words she began to crawl towards me. I was alarmed in case she bumped into something. 'Keep very quiet, won't you? Don't say a word,' I cautioned.

We stood together in the cooler air and I heard her gulp in mouthfuls. I could see she was shorter than me and could easily hide in the gaps between the chests. The moonlight on her hair showed it to be chestnut colour, not black. She looked up into my face and smiled – a smile that showed not one tooth missing. Something happened to my heart, I didn't want that moment to end. I heard myself whisper hoarsely, 'Better get back now.' I saw her nod and when we were safely under the sheet again, she whispered, 'Thank you.'

I was just about to leave her when I remembered I wanted to ask her something. 'Why do you want to go to London? It's an awful place, especially for girls.'

'It can't be worse than them I'm leaving, can it?' She was silent for a moment and I waited. 'My uncle...' Fiercely she went on, 'How can he be my uncle? No real uncle would behave like he did.'

'What do you mean?'

'How old are you?' she asked.

'Why?'

'You're too young to know how awful some people can be.'

'I'm not that young.' Again I had to wait for her to speak.

'My uncle thought to teach me about being married.'

'You mean cleaning and cooking?'

'Something like that.' She sniffed. 'Two dreadful men wanting me.' I wasn't sure what she meant by that but if the men were bad she had to get away. I made up my mind, I would do my best to get her to London no matter what Pa might do to me.

Next day as usual, I was kept busy and had no opportunity to see Martha. I began to worry about her being thirsty, so I dipped my mug into the pitcher of fresh water, took a sip and when I was yelled for I left it on deck close to the loose corner of the sheet.

There had been a bit of a fuss in the afternoon, the little uns couldn't find Puss. Normally she would be stretched out in the sunshine or prowling about the boat or on Nellie's back. They called and called fruitlessly hour after hour, but I was sure I knew where Puss was.

Puss turned up safely at suppertime. During the meal I hid a wedge of bread and a cold piece of bacon in my loose shirt, hoping to give it to Martha later. After Pa had finished his second mug of tea, with a generous spoonful of condensed milk in it, he surprised everyone by saying, 'You know what ma, I do believe it's Ned's birthday.' Ma looked at the length of shadows on the bank.

'I do believe you're right, Pa,' she said.

'In that case, I must be eighteen or nineteen,' declared Ned. Pa and Ma nodded together. Ned was their first child born soon after their marriage in 1897 or thereabouts.

'Probably eighteen I should reckon,' said Pa.

'So it's about time I had me own boat.'

'Not 'til your twenty-one, son.'

'Look at me pa. Don't I look twenty-one? Anyone would think I was twenty-one and I know everything you taught me.' I heard Pa sigh.

'Aye, I suppose you're right.' Pa looked across to ma. 'What do you think missus? Look for a boat for him next time we in Stoke?'

'And lose another of my chillen?'

'It's time, and one less mouth to feed. It's time he was a man of his own.' Pa's word was law.

Ned grinned with satisfaction; he looked round at all the faces smiling at him. I saw him take a swallow. 'I'll miss you all of course, you specially ma.' There were murmurs from around the table. I, for one, would miss him, as it would mean a lot more work for me when he left.

'As I see it,' he went on, 'I best get me a missus of my own and have an army of little uns then I won't be so lonely.'

'Now, steady on, son.' There was a note of caution in pa's voice. 'You got to get some standing among the boat people first. Can't just go off and snatch a wench. First things first. A boat maybe, at our next calling, but nothing else for the time being.' I believe Ned was satisfied – he was to get his own boat at last.

When I finally got to Martha, I was pleased she had drunk the water. 'I guessed you had left it on purpose,' she said.

I handed her the food I'd saved and she ate it down fast. 'Well, you soon ate that. Sorry that's all there is. I'll try to bring more tomorrow.' As usual our conversations were in whispers. 'Pa will be mad if he ever finds out about you.'

She gave a quiet chuckle. 'Yes, I've heard him bawling for you. I wouldn't like to cross him. No, not one little bit.'

'Look out for water tomorrow and don't worry you'll get to London soon.' As I left her, I saw Puss creep in and snuggle up to her and heard her purring.

During the night the breeze had strengthened and everyone was glad for it. The routine was the same as usual, but interrupted round noon. I was leading Nellie and Ned was aboard talking to Ma and drinking a brew, he liked his very strong. I heard Pa call out, 'The tarp's lifting in one corner, Ned. See to it. Fasten it down firmly.'

I went cold, what if Ned discovered Martha? Once the tarp was fastened, would Martha be able to breathe? Would I find her dead this night? It was only midday, hours away from supper. All day I fretted. I knew I had to get Martha out of her hiding place and face the consequences.

After supper, Ned sat on the cabin roof and smoked. Ma scolded him and although I was uneasy and struggling with the problem of saving Martha, I laughed when he said, 'I'm twenty-one now, ma. Pa agreed,' and in the fading light I saw him wink at me. Ned decided he too, like me, would sleep outside. I waited and waited until finally he was asleep.

'Martha, Martha,' I whispered as loudly as I dared. 'Where are you?'

Her voice was full of sleep when she answered. 'With the cat, over here.'

I made my way to her, gave her food and told her she must leave. 'We are only a day or so now, from London,' I told her. 'You will have to watch for a chance to get on the bank, probably at supper time. We all eat together at that time. You could creep out then.'

'You've been so good, Bert. I'll do as you say, but I don't want to get you into trouble.'

'If you're caught just don't say I helped you.'

She grasped my hand. 'Thank you Bert,' and I left her, hoping the plan would work.

I crept back to sleep beside Ned, but he was wide awake. 'Where have you been?'

'Growing hedges,' I answered. That's what we say when we need to wee.

'No, you haven't. I saw you in the hold. What you been up to?'

'Checking you fixed the tarp.'

Ned was quiet and I thought he was satisfied with the answer, but he twisted my arm. 'You're up to something. You're messing with the cargo and hoping to sell a few bone china cups to the lock-keeper's missus.'

I wanted to moan out loud with the pain he was causing me. Instead I groaned softly, 'No, I'm not.' He dragged me to my feet.

In a low voice he said, 'Keep your noise down,' and pulled me after him down on to deck then along to the cargo hold.

'Wait,' I pleaded. 'Wait, and I'll tell you.' He stopped.

'Go on then, start talking.'

And suddenly an idea came into my head – a really brilliant idea. 'It's your birthday present.'

'You're soft in the head.'

'There's a stowaway...'

Before I could say anything further he had shouted out, 'A bloody stowaway? Pa will kill you.' He shook me until my teeth rattled. 'You silly little fool.'

'It's a girl,' I felt like crying, but held back my tears.

'I don't care if it's the king of France.'

'I thought she could be your missus.'

There was mighty roar – Pa had woken up. He stomped out of the cabin pulling his braces over his shoulders.

'It's a stowaway, Pa,' Ned said quietly.

'Ma, a lamp, now,' Pa bellowed. Then he began swearing and threatening. I stood behind Ned.

'You're blaspheming in front of the boys, Bert,' Ma said as she handed the lamp over. Pa muttered something. I could see his face in the lamplight, red and screwed up with anger, ugly and frightening.

Still muttering he half turned to ma, 'A brew would be handy,' he said as he strode off to the hold.

Within a couple of minutes, I heard Martha shouting, 'Get off me. Leave me alone,' as Pa, with his hand clamped around her wrist, dragged her towards us. I stepped towards her, but she gave me a warning look and I stayed at Ned's side. In the lamplight I could see she was untidy and dirty, but very pretty. I glanced at Ned who he was looking at her. I could see he was surprised. Martha looked defiantly back at him and he flushed. He gave her a brief smile and I could see he was embarrassed as he turned away. I knew for sure that something had happened to his heart just like mine.

Pa turned to Ned, who shook his head and said, 'I know nothing about this.' Pa turned to me and something serious happened to my heart again. It sank, sank through the deck and down through the murky water.

It was Ma who saved me. 'Here we are,' she said handing round the mugs. 'She ain't going anywhere, Bert. Let her be.' Pa let go of Martha. 'Now then, girl, what's going on here? You after one of my boys?' she asked.

Martha glared at her. 'I've had enough of the likes of them for a lifetime,' she snapped.

'Hoity toity.' Ma turned to Pa. 'Best sleep on this I reckon. We'll sort her out in the morning.' Pa was astounded by what she said next. 'You sleep on the top with the lads, I'll keep an eye on this one. No nonsense on this boat, you can be sure.'

Pa didn't protest. 'We know nothing about this thief.' He stroked his chin for a moment, and then said, 'Could be the daughter of a lord or someone. You're right. We'll take care of things, and him,' he pointed at me, breathing deeply before saying, 'IN THE MORNING.'

Ned and I overslept until gone six. When we woke we looked at each other and Ned said, 'More trouble with Pa, for us then.' It wasn't so as Pa and Ma had started work at the usual time, around four-thirty in the summer. One of the little ones was leading Nellie. The towpath was straight and we wouldn't reach another lock for a good half hour so a bit of practice wouldn't do her any harm. We were surprised to see Martha in the cabin in one of ma's skirts, far too large, and mending her own dress. When she saw us she smiled and hurried to the stove and began our breakfast.

Ma and Pa were at the tiller talking and they looked serious. Ma was looking up into his face and Pa was looking cross about something. When he gave a couple of definite nods Ma left him, smiling to herself.

Ma came into the cabin and went across to Martha, 'Well done, girl.' She turned to us. 'Seems, this poor child has had a bad time of it and threatened with all sorts.' Ma beamed, she was obviously pleased about something, 'so Pa has said we will get her safely to London.' I guessed why Ma was happy. She was missing Lizzy, my sister, about the same age as Martha. For a few hours at least, she had a grown up daughter to chat with. I watched Ned. He kept looking at Martha who seemed, all of a sudden, to be very shy. Ma shooed Ned out. 'Find yourself some work,' she told him. For the next few hours, it seemed to me that Ned found excuses to see Martha but Ma kept an eye on her all the time.

Reaching the lock, I jumped down to open the gates, Ned uncoupled Nellie and Pa stood at the tiller waiting patiently for the water in the lock to lower. All of us were busy, so I was surprised when a large man on a horse, cantered up. 'Hi, there captain,' he called out to Pa.

'Good day, to you sir,' I heard Pa answer.

'You're about your business I see,' the fellow said. I heard him clear his throat. 'I've two guineas here if you've a mind to help.'

I saw Pa shrug. 'Depends.'

The man dismounted and waited smoking a large cigar until the boat was once again level with the banks.

'Sorry to trouble you,' he said when Pa finally stood beside him. Ned and I decided to see what the fellow was after.

The man coughed again, appearing a bit uncomfortable I thought. He threw his half-finished cigar into the canal. 'I'm looking for a girl...' I thought Pa was going to hit him when I saw his fists. 'No, no,' the man protested seeing pa's reaction, 'Not what you are thinking, my friend.' He smiled. 'No the girl I'm looking for is named Martha who has run away from her loving family.'

I felt Ned stiffen beside me. Pa looked at the ground then up into the man's face.

'No,' and he turned.

Everything changed suddenly. Martha came out of the cabin and called, 'Brew's ready.'

The man swung round at her voice. 'That girl.' He was pointing at Martha. 'You lied, you rogue,' he shouted at Pa. 'Get yourself down here, now, you bitch.'

Ned quickly leapt aboard and stood in front of Martha and Ma rushed out of the cabin. Pa, a good four inches shorter than the man, placed himself firmly in front of the man looking ready for a fight.

'We don't talk like that to our womenfolk,' Pa told him. His quiet tone seemed to enrage the man more.

'She's trouble.' He pointed at Martha. 'She belongs with us. We take good care of her.'

Pa shook his head gently and there was as a smile of disbelief on his face. 'So, I've heard. If you please, sir,' Pa did not give the customary salute when addressing his betters, 'tell me why she is so keen to leave such a...a loving family as you say?'

This seemed to stump the fellow for a second or two; he took a step towards Pa and looked down into his face, 'I can think of no reason.'

'Oh, there must have been a reason, sir. Why else would she be at the canal side?'

'What do you mean? She was to be wed to my friend, someone with money who would look after her for the rest of her life.'

'Did she choose him?'

'It's a family arrangement.'

'Ah,' Pa sighed loudly. 'I understand now.'

'Get yourself here, now,' he yelled at Martha.

'If my boys had not helped her…' I heard Ma say, so very solemnly, 'A mortal sin there'd be on your conscience, sir.' Ma had a bit of book learning and knew about these church matters.

'She's to come with me.' The man was quieter now as that news seemed to have unnerved him.

Pa rarely lied, but what he said next was a real whopper. He put his thumbs in his braces and started a fresh lie, bigger than Ma's.

'I think not sir. Her husband wouldn't allow it.'

'Husband?' bellowed the man.

'My son married her, yesterday – a boat people's wedding. We ain't got time for churches and suchlike.'

I didn't know who to look at first, my head swivelling from person to person. Ned was grinning as he stepped beside Martha, took her hand and didn't he just lean down to kiss her forehead. Martha was looking at the floor and had gone very red, and ma's jaw had fallen and her eyes were open wide. The man had raised his whip. 'I'll have the law on you, you cur,' he blustered. 'Abduction, that's what this is. Abduction! Prison, for the lot of you.'

'And you'll be joining us if you use that whip. Grievous bodily harm, I reckon.' The man dropped his arm and began muttering and turned to his horse as dad patted Nellie's behind and ordered, 'Walk on.'

Pa came aboard and the little un was leading Nellie again. 'Thanks, pa,' Ned said.

'Aye, don't get any ideas.'

'No,' Ma said fiercely and grabbed Martha away from Ned. 'You stay by my side until we dock. You understand?' She turned to Ned, 'and you stay away from her or else I'll see Pa give you a walloping you'll take scares of for the rest of your life.'

'But Ma,' I'd never heard Ned wail like that before.

'Leave it, son,' Pa said, 'we'll see what's what when we meet up with that vicar chap that did for me and your Ma.'

Ned grinned, 'I'll not change my mind, I'm thinking,' he said.

No wonder he was happy, eighteen or twenty-one, it didn't matter, he was going to see about a boat of his own with a brand new missus, and if he didn't marry Martha, I would when I was older.

THE END

## A Friendship Tested

Rachel was usually one of the first to arrive at the Saturday Drama Group, but today she had been held up. When she arrived, her friends, Daisy, Hannah and Amber were already there.

'Hi,' she called out as she entered. 'How's everyone? Learned your lines yet?' She put down her holdall, sat on the bench and looked at her group of friends. She was a little surprised that no one had answered. Usually there were cheery return greetings and one or more of them would rush over and begin telling her of the latest boyfriend or a trendy lipstick. Sometimes there was an invite to MacDonald's or a party. She leaned down to fish out a tissue from her bag. When she lifted her head and pushed up her glasses that had slid down her nose, she saw her friends were in a huddle whispering with their backs to her.

Rachel frowned. It looked as if they were deliberately ignoring her and she felt a little uneasy. Trying to shake off the feeling she stood, took a deep breath and telling herself she was imagining things walked across to them. 'What's up?' she said as she slipped a friendly arm around Daisy's waist. Immediately Rachel felt Daisy stiffen and move away from her. The feeling of unease increased and tentatively she said, 'Daisy?'

Amber's dark, straight hair fluttered around her face as she swung her head away.

Daisy deliberately cupped her ear.

'Did any of you hear something?' Amber and Hannah shook their heads.

'I do believe we have an ex friend here. Sorry, I meant someone we thought was our friend.'

Rachel was bewildered. 'I am,' she exclaimed. 'I am. We've been friends since High School.' Almost in tears she looked from one to another. What's changed? What have I done? she thought. No one spoke until whispering began among the three girls and Rachel, with heavy feet, walked back to the bench and sat down.

Daisy and Rachel had started at Grayborough High School together. At eleven years of age Rachel had been plump and shy. Daisy, full of confidence, had sat beside her in the hall waiting for the Head's Welcome Speech.

Daisy had smiled as she asked, 'What's your name? Whose class are you in?'

Rachel remembered she had gone hot. No one usually took any notice of her. If they did it was only to make some remark about her glasses or weight. Long ago in the Infants she had learned to cope – usually she laughed as her dad had advised. 'Try to make them your friend. Ignore what they say. You'll see, when you grow up you'll be more beautiful than any of them.'

'Rachel,' she mumbled back.

Daisy had laughed. 'Don't talk to your boots. Look at me.' Rachel lifted her head and heard the admiration in Daisy's voice. 'My word, you have the bluest eyes I've ever seen.'

A smile lit up Rachel's face.

'That's better,' Daisy said. 'My sister said that the first day at a new school is always the worst so find a friend immediately so that you won't feel lonely.'

Rachel couldn't believe it; someone ready to make friends with her on the first day. The few friends she had at Junior School had gone to different High Schools and Rachel had been dreading this day all the summer holidays. 'Sounds like a good idea.'

'Yes it is and I've chosen you. Rachel, you said?' Rachel nodded. 'So who's your form teacher?'

'Mrs Roberts.'

'Same as me! That's settles it then. Shake hands.' From that moment, four years ago, they had been firm friends.

They had become friends with Hannah and Amber two years later at the Saturday Drama Club. Hannah had muffed her lines in a play being rehearsed for a public showing at the local theatre. Everyone was excited as it was their first public performance. The Director, John Ryan, had been fierce, demanding the very best from everyone and they all knew that he was pleased at their improving standards. That is until Hannah had faltered.

'Hannah,' he had yelled. 'You've had three weeks to learn your lines. Is it too much to ask? Surely you know them?' Everyone watched Hannah crumple at his words and she ran off the stage to the cloakroom.

Amber had run after her shouting her name.

Daisy nudged Rachel. 'What a pig. I've a good mind not to be in his play. Come on let's see if we can cheer Hannah up.'

'Of course we must. My art teacher always made rotten comments about my paintings so I know how she feels.'

Daisy grabbed Rachel's arm and dragged her towards the cloakroom, laughing at the same time as she said, 'Yes, and I know why.'

As they crossed the hall they heard John say, 'Sorry, sorry everyone. I get carried away sometimes.'

They found Hannah in a cubicle seated on the lavatory. She was sobbing into her hands and Amber had her arm around her shoulders trying to comfort her.

'Do you know your lines?' demanded Daisy.

'Of course she does.' Amber snapped and Hannah nodded at the same time.

'So?'

Lifting her tear stained face, Hannah sobbed, 'So what? I can't...'

'Oh yes you can. Come on. Get out there and show that egomaniac you can do it.'

Hannah shook her head, 'I can't.' As she said this Daisy and Rachel were already pulling her to her feet.

'Yes you can, and afterwards we'll go to MacDonald's and really assassinate his teaching abilities.'

Amber and Rachel laughed and Hannah gave a weak smile.

'If he doesn't give you a chance or says just one word of criticism well... I'm not sure what we'll do.'

'We can all forget our lines. That would really put him in a dilemma,' Amber suggested.

'Brilliant, let's go,' and Daisy led them back into the hall. From that day forward the four girls had been inseparable. But now?

The door swung open again and again as other students arrived and it seemed to Rachel, all with friends laughing and chattering. A couple of girls made their way over to where Daisy and the others were standing. A hot embarrassing feeling came over Rachel when they all turned their backs on her, but surreptitiously kept glancing over their shoulders in her direction. Her eyes brimmed with tears and she felt like digging a hole in the middle of the floor and jumping in.

Rachel bounced as someone thumped down beside her. Quickly brushing away the tears she turned to see who it was.

''Wow, get a load of that,' he exclaimed pointing at the scenery. 'See what can be done in a week! He turned to her, 'Great isn't it?'

Rachel looked into his cheery face and her spirits lifted. Tom, so tall that he'd earned the nickname Lanky, didn't seem to mind being teased. Already he had made her feel better. 'Yes, yes it is. Just look at the way Dave's done the sea.'

'It looks like just a few strokes of white and green and hey presto. That guy's a wizard.' He slid along the bench so that he was almost touching her. 'Now that you're on your own…' he began. 'Why is it that you lot are always in a huddle? No one can get anywhere near any of you.'

'We, I…' Hannah faltered.

'Oh, never mind. I was wondering if you'd like to watch me play this afters? Down at the rec.' He glanced at her face. 'You alright? Not got a cold or anything? Your eyes are a bit red and you're sniffing.'

'I'm fine,' she replied forcing herself to smile. 'A bit of dust I think in my eye.' She looked across again to her friends, stood up and said, 'Excuse me a mo. There's something I've got to do.'

'I'm in the winning team,' he called as she began to move away and she heard him chuckle.

As she walked across the hall she was pleased Tom had spoken to her. She was grateful for his friendly chatter. Somehow this had given her the determination she needed to approach the three girls. This confidence was shaken when she watched them nudge and give knowing smiles to each other as she approached. Somehow Rachel knew she had to find out what had caused them to turn against her so suddenly.

She felt herself go hot when she reached them. 'Tell me what's up? What have I done to upset you lot?' she asked.

In a firm tone Daisy spoke. 'Remember girls, we are not going to speak to ...this snobby pig ever again.'

Rachel was shocked at the hostility in her voice. 'But what...? Tell me.'

'What did you say this ex friend of yours did Daisy?'

'Yes, what have I ever...' began Rachel.

Daisy's eyes widened. 'Look, she's trying to talk to me. Can't she take a hint?'

The three girls clustered together making sure Rachel was not included but could hear.

'So, Daisy what exactly did she do?'

In a resigned, but loud voice Daisy said, 'As I said before, I was walking along the High Street this morning and I saw HER coming towards me with her mother and when I said "Hello" her nose went up in the air and she ignored me completely. Cut me dead as if I didn't exist.' Her acting skills took over. She took a tissue out of her sleeve and wiped her eyes and almost sobbing added, 'and I was her best friend. Forever, we said.'

Rachel took a step towards them. 'But I never saw you. I didn't have my glasses on.'

Amber sniffed, 'At least she could have said hello back.'

'But it is so noisy in the High Street and mother was...' By now others had come across to the group and Rachel was almost in tears. 'Why won't you listen to me?'

'We're agreed then. That person is no longer our friend.' Amber and Hannah nodded.

Amber was thoughtful and pursed her lips. 'Shame in a way.'

'What do you mean? She...'

'I mean... Well girls, just look at her brother. Such a dishy guy.'

In a dreamy tone Hannah sighed. 'Joe! Yes, you've got a point. That's something I can't understand. I mean, Joe. Just look at him so good looking and friendly and her so gross. I suppose we could...'

Daisy sharply interrupted. 'No we couldn't. It would mean having to talk to HER politely if he dates one of us.' She paused for a moment. 'He says he rather fancies…' Amber and Hannah looked at her expectantly but she shrugged her shoulders leaving them wondering who?

With her stomach churning Rachel had heard enough and stumbled her way to the bench. Two thoughts came into her head, first such a trivial excuse to fall out with her and why wouldn't they give her a chance to explain? Sighing, she took a book out of her bag, ignoring the tissues that she badly wanted to wipe away the tears of frustration on her cheeks. No, she wouldn't give them the satisfaction of thinking she was crying. She didn't get a chance to open her book.

Tom had returned. 'Fallen out?'

She nodded.

'So? You coming then, this afternoon?'

John had arrived and clapped his hands. Everyone stopped what they were doing, then there was an immediate rush to their places when he called out, 'We all ready then?'

As Rachel and Tom made their way to the stage she said, 'I'll be there, I'll have to cheer Joe though.'

Tom laughed. 'He's in my team so you'd better.'

Monday, a school day and Rachel toyed with the idea of pleading sick or having a headache in order to take the day off. Hoping that everything would soon be back to normal, she had said little to Joe and said nothing at all to her parents about the quarrel. No, she thought, if I stay away the girls might think they had upset me. Well yes, they had but she was aching to put matters right.

It was obvious from the moment she reached the school gates when Daisy, Hannah and Amber had coolly turned away that they were determined to exclude her. Bravely, Rachel talked and laughed with the other students, but in some ways she felt quite lonely as she missed her friends.

Every morning when Rachel woke, she hoped this would be the day when, perhaps one of the trio would speak.

Thursday, and she had a date with Tom. They were going to the cinema. It was Daisy who had schooled her in the art of using make-up so that her mascara didn't run and a touch of colour on the cheeks to highlight her face. 'There,' Daisy had said one evening gently brushing on a pale lipstick, 'Perfect.' The plumpness that had plagued Rachel through junior school had disappeared and her confidence had grown.

After the football match last Saturday, she had stood with Joe on the side-line and Tom with his usual beaming face came across to them. 'Told you, didn't I? Told you, I'd be on the winning team.'

Rachel nodded.

Joe laughed, 'Pity you didn't score a goal then. You just ran up and down the field like a soppy puppy.'

Joe swung his body about and pouted. 'Nobody gave me a chance.' and then cheerfully thumped Joe on the shoulder. 'Hey, a good game though, wasn't it?'

'An easy win if you ask me. That team was rubbish.' Joe turned to Rachel. 'Come on you, let's go. I want a shower and I'm starving.'

Tom put out his hand and held Rachel back. 'Hang on a mo.' Joe raised his eyebrows. 'Not you, you idiot.'

Joe gave a knowing 'Ah,' and walked away as Tom turned to Rachel.

'I was wondering…' he hesitated then blurted out, 'Shall we, will you, er…'

Bemused Rachel asked, 'What?' and watched Tom swallow quickly.

'Thursday? How about coming to the cinema with me?'

Thursday started well enough, she was pleased when her teacher had taken her aside and praised her essay, but she was uneasy when she turned and saw Amber had overheard his praises.

At lunch time she saw Amber, Daisy and Hannah sitting together. There was only one seat available – too close to the three. Rachel didn't hesitate and sat down in time to hear Amber say, 'One thing I do miss not speaking to…' giving a nod in Rachel's direction, 'you know who. She was pretty good at helping me with my French homework.'

Hannah sniffed, 'She's nothing but a swot and a snob.'

Daisy added, 'And a teacher's pet.'

Rachel fumbled in her bag for her book desperate to ignore their taunts.

'Look, look at her. I bet she's swotting up now. Bet she thinks she's good enough for uni.' Rachel was startled when suddenly the book was snatched out of her hands. 'See, I was right. She's reading...' Daisy turned the book over losing Rachel's place while she scanned the title. 'She's reading...' Her voice raised into an unbelieving shriek. 'Shakespeare!'

Amber shrugged her shoulders. 'So what? If she goes to uni we won't have to look at her ugly face again.'

Rachel took a deep breath and with her face flushed she turned to the mean little group. 'I'm not a snob. I want us to be friends again.'

Daisy gave a rude snort.

Rachel ignored it and continued. 'I wish you'd listen to me. I just didn't see Dai...' before she could finish the girls stood up and left her open mouthed. It's so not fair, she muttered to herself.

Some students had gathered in the library. Most of them were clustered around Mia who was frantically searching through her bag and wailing, 'My phone. Oh God, where's my phone?' One boy lifted a mountain of papers from the desk, someone rummaged through the wastepaper basket, another checked the librarian's desk and others began asking around. There was no doubt, the phone was missing.

Angrily Mia glared around. 'Someone's stolen my phone,' she shouted, 'Come on, own up.'

In a soothing tone Rachel said, 'Don't say that. Say something like, someone's borrowed my phone without asking. To say someone stole it is a bit unkind especially as we're,' she looked around then sighed, 'all friends.'

"I don't care! I just want my phone back. My dad will kill me if it's gone missing,' was the sullen reply.

'Come on, everybody, let's all have a good look round. It must be somewhere,' Hannah said.

There was a frenzy of activity for a few minutes as everyone searched and checked and checked again and again. Everyone noticed Mia's brimming eyes as she asked anxiously, 'Has anyone found it yet?' There was murmuring and a shaking of heads and she began to cry.

Rachel went across to console her and as she crossed the room heard

Amber say, 'Well, it's no good just standing around. If one of us has taken it, it should be easy to find out who.'

There was a shuffling of feet and everyone looked at each other. 'And how do you think you are going to do that?' a voice queried.

'By asking – who hasn't got a mobile?'

Hannah sniffed and Rachel gasped when she heard her say, 'Rachel hasn't got a mobile.'

Rachel angrily strode across to Hannah and staring into her eyes said, 'Are you accusing me Hannah Wilson?' She turned to face the students who had drawn closer. 'I do have a mobile.' She drew it out of bag. 'See, my dad bought it for me and I can honestly say it isn't me who took Mia's.' She took a deep breath. 'But it could be Hannah.' She hated herself for making the accusation, but no way was she going to be thought of as a thief.

Hannah's face went red. 'Don't you dare say that.' She turned to Daisy and Amber. 'Tell her, all of them – it isn't me.'

Rachel shrugged. 'It could be you. You haven't got a phone yet. You told me you were getting one for your birthday.'

A distant bell was heard and there was a flurry of people rushing to the door. Mia gave a last frantic look around the room and muttered to no one in particular, 'I thought I put it on the table. I can't remember now, but I daren't go home without it. I'll be grounded forever, I know I will.'

Rachel shrugged off her coat as she entered the hall a few Saturdays later. It was raining heavily and she was glad Joe had given her a lift. She smiled to herself knowing how pleased he was for the chance to show off his driving skills now that he had his driving licence. Dad had been reluctant to loan his car, but seeing the heavy rain had given in to their pleas.

It had been necessary for Daisy, Hannah and Amber to work alongside Rachel over the last few weeks. There were projects at school that all four were involved with. Rachel did her best to avoid them in the playground and lunchtimes. This seemed to work. They ignored her and the mean rumours were no longer as spiteful. All still attended the Saturday drama sessions, but the coolness between them remained. Rachel had come to terms with the situation and didn't give into tears. She was determined not to let it get her down, but yes, she admitted to herself that she missed them as friends.

'Take care, everyone,' John warned when he arrived. 'The floor is very slippery in the cloakrooms. Don't want any accidents.' The rehearsal went smoothly, everyone knew their parts now and with some instructions from John, the play was beginning to look polished. At the end of the two-hour session he was full of praise. 'Well done everyone.'

Amber muttered, 'That's a first,' and someone giggled.

John frowned then smiled. 'I know I've been a bit hard on some of you. But…' he paused, then spread his arms as if to embrace them all. 'just look at how well everything is going. Everyone deserves a pat on the back.' He gave a chuckle, 'I wouldn't be surprised if some of you end up in a play in the West End one day.' Everyone was smiling and thumbs were raised. 'Right, same time next week. Off you go,' he commanded.

There was chattering and laughter as people collected their coats and bags and left. Joe said he would pick Rachel up and she waited patiently in the foyer hoping he wouldn't be long. She thought she was the last one to leave and was surprised to hear a sudden shout from the girls' changing room. This was followed by someone moaning. Rachel put down her bags and hurried to see what had happened. When she opened the door she was surprised to see Daisy, her face screwed up in pain, clutching her arm and struggling to get up off the floor. Rachel rushed across to help her. 'What happened?' she asked as she put her arm around Daisy's waist to steady her and lead her to a bench.

Daisy leaned back against the wall and shut her eyes. 'I…I slipped on the wet floor,' she whispered. 'I was in a hurry and just…' she tried to move her arm and gasped. 'I think it's broken,' she whimpered. 'Oh, Rachel, the pain is so…so awful,' and she began to cry.

'Don't say that. I hope you're wrong. Perhaps it's just a sprain.'

'It's more than that, I can tell.'

'In that case,' Rachel said briskly and heading for the door. 'I'll get Joe. He can take us to the hospital.'

'Joe?'

'Yes, he's meeting me. Wait there,' and she hurried away.

In a few minutes she returned with Joe.

'Jeez!' Joe exclaimed. 'You're as white as a ghost! I wouldn't like to meet you on a dark night.'

'Come on Daisy, stand up and we can help you to the car,' Rachel said as she put her arm around Daisy. As Daisy stood her legs gave way and she immediately began to crumple. Quickly Joe grabbed her and sat her down again.

Concerned, he looked down on her, then gently took her good hand. 'We'll wait a few seconds then try again shall we? I'll look after you, I promise.' With Daisy between them they walked through the hall to the car, enlivened by Joe's attempts to make her smile.

Although said in jest, when he said, 'I've waited a long time to put my arms around you,' Rachel was astounded and Daisy raised her eyebrows as she said, 'Really?' They had reached the car and there was no time for Joe to answer.

Rachel and Joe waited the two long hours it took for Daisy to be seen and treated. When she finally returned with her arm in a sling, she had regained her colour and was smiling. 'Thanks for waiting. There was no need really, but I'm so glad you did.'

'Come on,' Joe said taking her good arm, 'let's get you home. It's way past lunch and I'm starving.'

As Joe helped her out of the car outside her home he said, 'Why don't you join me and Tom and her…' he pointed rudely to his sister. 'We're going bowling tonight. You might enjoy it.' Both girls began to giggle then laughed outright. Bewildered Joe asked, 'What? What?'

'You silly blighter,' Rachel spluttered. 'How, tell us how is she going to bowl?'

Joe clapped his hand to his forehead and rolled his eyes. 'Sorry, sorry Daisy. I just thought it would be great if we all went together.'

Unsure, Daisy looked at Rachel before saying, 'I'll come and watch if you like.' She turned to Daisy. 'That is if it's alright with you, Rach?'

'Alright by me,' was the reply.

Joe sniffed. 'Well if it isn't, that's too bad. I'm sure me and Daisy will get on fine without you.' As Daisy made her way to her door, he called after her, 'Pick you up around seven. Okay?'

Rachel sat out of the game to keep Daisy company who slid along the bench to her side. 'I'm so sorry we fell out,' she began. 'I was a real bitch to you, wasn't I?'

Rachel looked into Daisy's eyes. She nodded as she softly said, 'Yes.'

'I didn't mean to. I was having a bad time at home. Everyone was rushing about because my granddad had a heart attack.'

Rachel's hand flew to her mouth. 'The one who always teases us? Is he alright?'

'That's so like you, Rachel. So kind and yes, he's much better now. At the time my mother was crying, thinking he was going to die, and Nan needed her to take her to the hospital and well…well it seemed, somehow overwhelming. Everyone was so scared. I didn't know what to think or what to do. I was all over the place and took it out on you. I am truly sorry.'

Full of concern for her friend, Rachel took Daisy's hand. 'You should have said. You know I was…' she smiled at Daisy, 'am always there for you.'

Swinging their joined hands up into the air, Rachel said, 'Oh, shut up. Come on tell me all the news. I've missed our girly chats.'

'Me too.'

'Tell me where did Mia find her phone in the end?' Rachel asked. 'I see she's got it back or did she have to get a new one?'

'Don't you know?' Rachel shook her head.

'She'd gone to the library to get some books for her project and put a pile of them on the table.' Joe and Tom had finished their game and joined them. 'What she hadn't realised was that she had put the books on top of the phone.'

'All that fuss,' Rachel exclaimed. 'It was so embarrassing, everyone accusing each other. I was really hurt.'

'Yes, sorry.'

Together, they drank cokes and dipped into crisp bags. Tom wiped his mouth with the back of his hand and asked, 'What was her project then?'

'You remember, Rachel, we had to choose an invention of the nineteenth century that is still important today.'

'Yes, I chose vaccination.'

'Well, Mia chose Alexander Bell.'

Tom spluttered, coughed and began to laugh.

Rachel punched his arm. 'What's so funny?'

Joe began to chuckle and Tom still laughing gasped out, 'You tell them, Joe.'

Joe took a deep breath. 'You said she was working on the inventor, Alexander Bell?' The girls nodded. 'Well...' he glanced at Tom and they both laughed out loud together. 'He...he invented the telephone!'

THE END

## At the College Gates

Lisa's stomach was turning and fluttering. She knew it was called having butterflies. It had happened every day this term where she was training to be a nursery nurse. Now it was the end of the term and there was going to be a concert, and Mary, Lisa's best friend was going to sing tonight. As Lisa walked towards the college gate she knew she could never take part in the concert. Lisa's family were musical but she was too shy to sing. She sighed and shook back her long hair. This was being blown about by the strong wind across her eyes, and into her mouth. It was the wind that was upsetting her today.

Earlier in the term a strong wind had been blowing just like the one today. At that time as Lisa passed a group of boys lounging and smoking at the college gates, the wind had caught her pleated skirt. The skirt billowed, then lifted – high enough to expose her panties. How the boys cheered and clapped. One boy had whistled a whistle Lisa was to hear again and again over the next few weeks. Lisa thought she would never forget that day. The lads couldn't have seen too much, but enough to see the top of her long slender legs. Screaming, she pulled her skirt down and ran to get away from their crude jokes.

Thinking about some of the jokes afterwards she knew they were childish and silly, but one lad, taller than the rest had called out to her, 'Hey, beautiful. You've got the longest legs I've ever seen. They must be worth a million.' Lisa had briefly noticed his smile and even white teeth. 'Just like Madonna's,' he'd laughed.

'Give over Steve. More like Batman's,' one lad called out. It was then that Lisa, her face red with embarrassment and holding back tears, had run away. Much later she thought that the boy called Steve had meant his remarks to be a compliment but she couldn't be sure.

Every day since then, she had seen Steve. Often she saw him by himself leaning against the wall outside the college as if waiting, but he never spoke and turned away from her. If he was with the other lads he would stop fooling around and give out his distinctive whistle as she approached. Then she saw the others give him a sly poke or whisper something that made them fall about laughing. Often, she noticed that Steve would flush up, shuffle his feet, shove his hands in his pockets or attempt to thump the offender.

It was Steve, a student in his last year, who caused Lisa's daily butterflies. She'd heard he'd done well in his exams and that he would be starting work with an engineering company next week. Today would be the last day she would be seeing him. As she approached the gates she hoped he would say something to her – anything would be fine, but a date would be perfect. Yes, there he was and with him was the usual crowd of boys joking and larking about.

Steve did speak to her and it was not what she was expecting. In a sing-song voice, he called out 'It's W.I.N.D.Y...' and she watched as the boys grinned and nudged each other. 'Well, show us your undies girl,' Steve shouted and loud laughter greeted this rude remark, 'We won't get another chance will we lads?'

Lisa, wishing she was somewhere else and hating him, hurried away. As she did so she saw Steve turn away and punch his fist into his other hand, his face screwed up and she knew he was upset by his silly remarks. She also realised it was too late to get to know him better. As she walked away she kept her head up but inside she was hurting.

Later that evening she set out for the concert. She told her mother that she was going to support Mary. 'I expect she's a bit nervous,' she said, 'I know I would be.' Backstage she searched everywhere for her friend and began to feel worried knowing Mary might be late. Suddenly the music teacher rushed up to her.

'Lisa,' he said, 'Mary's lost her voice. Too much practising, I think.' He grabbed her wrist. 'You could take her place.' As Lisa shook her head he said, 'Please I know your father. He says you sing well, but you don't like to sing in front of an audience.'

Again she shook her head, 'No, I can't. No, never,' she protested.

'Do it please,' he begged, 'Do it for Mary, for the college.' He tugged at her arm. 'You can do it, I know you can. Please, Lisa, please.' Lisa sighed, then slowly nodded. She knew the tune and words well enough. It would all be over in a few minutes she told herself.

At last it was her turn to step onto the stage. Trembling from head to foot she stood, clutching her hands together. The piano softly played the introduction and Lisa opened her mouth to sing. However, her mouth seemed dry and she only made a husky, raw sound in her throat. The audience stirred restlessly; to run away now would be dreadful but to stay was just as bad. Lisa looked over to the person playing the piano – Miss Smithers, one of her favourite tutors. Miss Smithers smiled encouragingly at her and whispered, 'Start again, dear. Take a deep breath.' The audience waited. The opening music softly filled the hall and Lisa began to sing. She sang a slow song of lost love, her voice perfectly in tune. She sang with deep feeling from the heart as if she knew the pain of losing a lover. When she came to the end there was complete silence. Lisa couldn't understand it and, bewildered, she looked across to Miss Smithers.

Suddenly there was a roar of clapping and cheering. She stood still, feeling pleased and no longer nervous as the applause seemed to go on and on. Over all the din there came a loud whistle from the back of the hall, a whistle Lisa knew well.

It was nearly dark when Lisa set out for home. For the second time that day she made her way to the college gates. There were no lads there leaning against the wall but as she passed, by a warm hand gently took hers. 'I'll walk you home,' said Steve softly. For a second time that evening Lisa's heart was full of song.

THE END

# *Something Will Turn up*

'Open it Karen,' her mother said anxiously. Karen turned the envelope over. Yes, it was from a well-known local business. Would it be 'yes' or 'no'? Quickly she opened it and read:

'Dear Miss Reynolds,

We were impressed with your recent exam results and your fine voluntary work. After much consideration we feel that as you have not yet gained experience in our field of work, we are unable to offer you the position'.

The letter ended wishing her well in her search for work.

It was over three months since Karen had left school and this was her sixth unsuccessful application and each rejection had eaten away at her confidence. The problem was that she really didn't know what she wanted to do and at interviews never showed enough enthusiasm for the job on offer.

By the look of disappointment on her face and drooping shoulders, her mother guessed the letter's contents. 'Never mind love,' she said as she put her arm around Karen's shoulder, 'something will turn up, you'll see.'

After lunch Karen made her way to the centre where volunteer people of all ages were allocated a variety of caring tasks. One of her regular jobs was shopping for an elderly lady who grumbled at the cost of things and always queried her change despite receipts. Sometimes she helped a young mother with four children under five and really enjoyed looking after the four-year-old twins.

Today, Karen was asked if she would visit a blind lady. 'Just make her some tea and read the newspaper to her,' he supervisor told her. 'She really likes having company.'

'Who is it?' a cultured voice called in answer to Karen's knock.

A teacher-type voice Karen thought, and sighed. Clever people always made her feel inadequate. 'I'm Karen, from the Centre, Mrs Boothroyd,' she called out. 'They said they'd phone you.'

Karen hesitated at the door of an uncluttered room and was surprised to see a well-dressed woman about fifty-five years old. Karen also noticed that Mrs Boothroyd had neatly groomed short hair and immaculate make-up. Her welcoming smile put Karen at ease immediately.

'Are you there Karen? Sit down, I'll just make us a cup of tea then you can do something for me.' She bustled into the kitchen confidently laying out mugs and a plate of biscuits.

'Er, I'm supposed to do that,' Karen volunteered as she followed Mrs Boothroyd into the kitchen and moved towards the fridge for milk.

Mrs Boothroyd stopped what she was doing for a moment. 'Just keep still dear, I'll get the job done quicker if I don't bump into you. Milk, sugar?'

Having settled themselves comfortably in the back room, Mrs Boothroyd leaned towards Karen. 'Now,' she said, 'what I would like you to do is look into my garden and tell me what you see. It's early March so start on the left from this window. Tell me what you see up to the back fence. Don't leave anything out.'

Karen was surprised at the request and also dismayed. 'Well I'll do my best, but I don't know the names of many plants. Anyway, there are only daffodils there at the moment.'

'Only daffodils!' exclaimed Mrs Boothroyd as she thumped the arm of her chair in mild exasperation 'Only daffodils! There are many varieties Karen. Try to describe them, start from the window.'

'Yellow,' said Karen promptly.

'Pale yellow?'

'No, buttercup yellow,' Karen replied.

'Good, and what colour is the trumpet, the bell protruding from the yellow petals?'

'Almost white with a narrow orange frill and the leaves are going a little brown at the tips.'

'Ah, frost burn,' Mrs Boothroyd explained. 'Next.'

Peering with more care now, Karen said, 'Sorry Mrs Boothroyd, I missed the violets just a small clump in front of the daffodils.'

'Oh, bless you. I'd forgotten about them. I could see once you know, so I can "see" what you tell me inside my head.' She gave two or three nods of her head before adding, 'I had a careless accident in the lab. I forgot to pull my goggles down. Large flask exploded on the Bunsen burner. I got a double whammy to my eyes; glass and boiling liquid. Just forgot.' They sat quietly for a few moments, one remembering the awfulness of her accident, the other just as shocked, remembering the golden rules of the science teacher – 'goggles and a safe flame'.

Then, quite briskly, Mrs Boothroyd said, 'What do you see next, dear?'

'I'll start on the left, the left side of the garden, shall I? Then across the back fence, and back again along the right side.' Karen suggested.

'Yes, that will be perfect.'

Karen did her best to describe what she saw and Mrs Boothroyd gently questioned and corrected her. At the end of the afternoon Karen asked, 'Would you like me to come again, Mrs Boothroyd? I have enjoyed being with you.'

Mrs Boothroyd beamed, 'That would be lovely, dear. Things change in the garden so quickly, you can keep me up to date.'

A twice weekly visit became a set routine and each week there were new varieties and colours in the garden. They smelled and touched them, all the while Mrs Boothroyd passing on tips and information. Karen's interest grew and gradually she began to identify some of the more unusual plants. A warm bond of friendship grew between them and Karen was invited to call Mrs Boothroyd by her first name – Daisy.

'No wonder you like flowers. I think I ought to be called Rose or Jasmine, now,' Karen said, 'I really love the flowers and plants in your garden.'

'And everywhere else, I hope,' was the reply. Together they laughingly agreed on Rose.

At the end of July, Karen waited impatiently for news of her latest application. When she finally received a reply, she felt she would burst with excitement. She outlined its contents to her mother then rushed off to share the news with Daisy.

'It's here, it's here,' Karen cried, and threw her arms around her friend.

'Listen, "We are pleased to offer you a three year Horticulture Course beginning twenty-ninth September. Students are expected…" Oh, Daisy, just a few months ago I was so miserable. Now thanks to you, I know what I want to do. Thank you, I've learned so much from you.'

Hugging Karen back, Daisy said in a teasing but thoughtful voice, 'How's your Latin dear?'


THE END

## Walk Through the Woods

Carol, my mother suggested a walk. 'Through the woods, we haven't been there for a long time,' she said. It was our favourite walk and I readily agreed. We pulled on our wellies and tucked a bottle of water into our pockets. We took Bonnie, the dog and as soon as we arrived she shot off chasing the squirrels. Carol and I sauntered our way along a well-trodden, muddy path that meandered between massive oaks, spindly hazels and grabbing brambles.

'Sit here a moment,' said Carol when we reached a fallen tree trunk. 'I have something to tell you.' Both of us reached for our water bottles and swallowed a mouthful. Carol took my hand and surprised, I looked at her.

She gave me a ghost of a smile and sighed. Softly, almost inaudibly she said, 'Your father and I are not your real parents.'

I gasped, then half laughed. 'Oh, mum,' I grinned at her. 'Every parent says that when their child has done something wrong, like as if they don't want to own them.' She squeezed my hand. 'Come on, then. What have I done this time?'

She remained quiet for a few moments before saying, 'You were fifteen last week. We made up our minds that if things didn't alter while you were with us, we would tell you on your birthday.'

An unknown feeling almost of fear gripped me and I felt myself going cold as I asked, 'What do you mean?'

Carol was still clinging to my hand and said, 'You are Elizabeth's child, my sister. She came home to your gran's from London one day with you, only a few days old, in her arms. She told us nothing, nothing at all, and left the next day. We searched for her and made enquiries, but she never came back for you, so Frank and I registered you as ours.'

I pulled my hand out of hers absolutely dumbfounded. There was no mistaking what she had said. All of sudden, I wasn't me anymore.

All sorts of thoughts raced through my mind. From this moment on I feared I had no father, mother, sisters or brother. In a moment they had become my uncle, aunt and cousins. 'We love you, Hannah, darling. You are and always will be our precious daughter. Please love, try to understand. We couldn't let you go to just anybody.'

For what like seemed an eternity neither of us spoke, then she said, 'Say something, Hannah. Nothing has or will change. You are our girl, our daughter.'

Now I was angry. I stood up quickly and walked back and fore before finally stopping in front of her. 'Why didn't you tell me from the start?' and before she could answer, I added, 'What a wicked thing to do abandon a baby – abandon me!'

'We, we…' began Carol.

'I heard the first time. Took pity on poor little, motherless me, didn't you? Not really yours am I?'

I heard her sigh, 'It wasn't like that at all. We…'

'I don't want to hear.' I snapped back. It was when I saw her stricken face that I sat down beside her. 'Sorry Mum,' I said softly, 'Didn't mean to hurt you. You're truly the best any girl could have.' We linked our fingers together and I put my head on her shoulder, 'Why didn't you tell me, though?'

'Because we were afraid of losing your love – your respect,' she replied. 'See how angry you were just now. We wondered, what would be the best for you and we decided to tell you on your fifteenth.'

For a few moments we sat quietly each with our own thoughts, then I said, 'I want to see…to see her, my birth mother.'

'Do you? Do you think that wise?'

'I need to see her, Mum. I need to understand why?' Carol nodded.

'Have you had any contact with her at all?'

'Well, I haven't seen her in a long while, but we do exchange Christmas cards so I have her address somewhere.'

I heard the bitterness in my voice as I asked, 'And I suppose she never asks after me?' Carol shook her head.

'And you never told her?'

'No, we thought as you grew, she might change her mind if she saw what a beautiful child you were. We loved you so much and just couldn't bear the idea of parting with you.'

'Tomorrow then, I will go and see her and give her a piece of my mind.'

'And I'll go with you.'

Elizabeth was only an hour's drive away it turned out. And when we reached Elizabeth's door the next day and before knocking, we hugged each other. 'It'll be alright, you'll see,' I whispered. When our knock was answered I was amazed to see a woman who, without doubt, had almost the same features as Carol, grandma and me.

Elizabeth's face registered her shock at seeing us and her hand flew to her mouth. 'What are you doing here? What do you want?'

I didn't hesitate. – 'I'm your daughter. Hannah.'

Elizabeth glanced quickly behind her and stared hard at Carol. 'Why, why have you done this?' she hissed at her. 'I have a family. They…no one knows of this…this girl. I want no trouble.'

Carol smiled and reached out to her sister. 'Oh come on Lizzie, It's time I met this family of yours.'

I felt my heart leap with excitement. 'Does that mean I might have brothers and sisters?' I asked. Elizabeth glared at me before nodding.

'In that case, I should like to meet them.'

'Come on, Liz, invite us in. We won't stay long,' Carol pleaded.

'No, I think not!' For a moment Elizabeth stood biting her lip and finally agreed. As she stepped aside to let us in she whispered, 'On one condition.'

I frowned and I asked, 'And what is that?'

'You do not, under any circumstances, tell who you are.' It was Carol who nodded.

'This way then,' and we followed her very stiff back until we reached the sitting room. She stopped for a moment and I saw the agonized look on her face as she opened the door I heard her hoarse whisper reminding us of the promise. We looked into the room and saw two girls around ten and twelve, giggling and wrestling a man to the floor, who was pleading for mercy.

Brightly, and twisting her fingers nervously, Elizabeth called out,

'Hey, behave you two. Look who's come to see you. Your aunt Carol and…and …'

And before she could say anything more I said, 'Her daughter, your big sister, Hannah.' No one spoke. I saw the man, her husband frown, then walk over to Elizabeth who had collapsed into a chair. I saw him bend over and put his arms around her. The elder of the two girls shyly asked, 'Really, truly? You are a secret sister?' I nodded. Then the pair of them launched themselves at me. They hopped from foot to foot with excitement and were full of questions. I answered as carefully as I could. I didn't want to hurt Elizabeth any more who was now smiling up into her husband's face. When it was time to leave, Carol said, 'Well, you can come and visit your sister whenever you like.'

'Yes,' I said, 'and we will take the dog for a long walk in the woods.'

I'm not sure if Elizabeth will ever truly accept me as her daughter but, in my mind, Carol and Frank are my true, loving parents.

46

## Acknowledgements

Megan Carter, who suggested we make a New Year's Resolution to 'go for it' and publish some of our work on our own. Megan's book is entitled, *Amazing Grace*, a short collection of verse.

Many thanks to Anne Samson for her encouraging support over many years. Without her help I may not have had over fifteen books and a number of plays published.

## About Beatrice

Beatrice Holloway is a playwright and author.

A retired teacher, between 2015 and 2022, Beatrice was the Children's Storyteller for Hillingdon Narrowboats Association which led her to write about canal life.

The London Borough of Hillingdon library service published two of her children's stories and awarded her with a Certificate of merit – 'In recognition of an outstanding contribution to the Arts'. Beatrice was also awarded a Lottery Grant to write a commissioned historical play: *Commoner to Coronet*.

For a full list of Beatrice's books, see page 4.

www.ingramcontent.com/pod-product-compliance
Lightning Source LLC
Chambersburg PA
CBHW070609180626
46817CB00005B/2066